LIMITED EDITION PRINTING

_190_ *of 200*

THE WHITE TROLL
AND THE RESCUE OF GLADIATOR

THE WHITE TROLL

AND THE RESCUE OF GLADIATOR

WRITTEN BY CALEB JACKSON

ILLUSTRATED BY NICK FAUBLE

Printed and bound in Canada by Art Bookbindery

www.ArtBookbindery.com

ISBN 978-0-9911389-0-6

DEDICATED TO
FRIENDSHIP

A Shout-Out of Thanks!

To our heroic Kickstarter pledgers – your belief in a young author and your willingness to give money to make the unique characters in my book come to life has helped make my dream come true! Thank you!

* Cynthea J. Amason
* Fran Andrews
* Brandi Buck
* Patricia Campbell
* Susan Compton
* Dr. William E. & Debra J. Cox
* Kaci Finney
* Mike & Sheila Galeotti
* Jessicca Garcia
* Leon Gladstone, Meg and Holden
* Lisa Gooding
* April (West) Hamilton
* Candice Jackson, Zachary & Madelyn
* Gary & Sandra Jackson
* Jonathan & Elisa Jackson, Adora & Titus
* Rick & Jeanine Jackson
* Virgil & Ella Jackson
* Olga Mancini
* Megan Masters
* Nicole Serio Merritt
* Bob & Linda Neilson

* CHRISTOPHER PLOURDE
* JEFF & SHAWNA QUADE, FLETCHER, MITCHELL, & ELLISON
* TONY ROSSI
* MARK & KANDIDA SABO
* MARCIA SCHAFER
* JANET SHARP
* KAT SHEVLIN
* KEN STEELE
* JULIE SUMMERS
* CASSIE TENGAN
* JEFF VERNON
* DUANE & KATHY WARD

Thanks!

- *NICK FAUBLE*, Illustrator – Bringing my imagination to life is no easy task, but you made it fun, look easy, and crazy good! Thank you for sitting on the airplane beside my grandma – White Troll, Bat Head, and the Gladiator are forever in your debt. You are exceptionally brilliant and talented! Website: NickFauble.com

- *CANDICE E. JACKSON*, Attorney at Law & *PATRICIA J. CAMPBELL*, Attorney at Law – you give me the best legal team a ten-year old could ever dream of having! I'm so grateful to have you on my side, always watching my back. I feel very safe! You are the coolest warm-hearted lawyers in the universe! Contact: Candice@CEJacksonlaw.com

- *JANET SHARP*, Author – You paved the way for me to get my book published! Thank you for transcribing my story from audio to typed manuscript. I'm grateful that your creative power with words has rubbed off on me. Thank you, Auntie Janet!

- *MICHAEL SCHACHT & ART BOOKBINDERY* – You make dreams come true every day for authors, but this is a first for me. From the very first phone call, your excitement and description of possibility was a huge boost. Thank you to you, Brendan, Yvonne, and the team! Website: artbookbindery.com

* *ALL MY FAMILY AND FRIENDS* — You give me constant support and encouragment! Through your words and example, I have developed a love for story and creative journey. I'm so thankful for your love and prayers. You know who you are!

* *JESUS* — I like the way You created me, and I am so grateful for Your daily gifts of inspiration, kindness, grace, friendship, and love. You are so good to me!

Contents

CHAPTER ONE
HOW THE WAR STARTED

THERE WERE MANY men living in the Gladiator's Kingdom. Everything was very happy in the Village. People were dancing, stuffing their faces, playing the game "who gets the most drunk" (which Gladiator had to stop or those people would have gone nuts), and having a great time—juggling, clowning around, kids laughing in the streets, playing with balls, falling in mud, scraping their knees—all kinds of fun stuff.

The Village had a big Celebration of their new King, the Gladiator, who was a very well known Hero in Gladiator's entire Kingdom.

They brought out Gladiator, walking like a real King with a new Robe, new Jewelry, a new Sword, all kinds of things, and everybody bowed to him gracefully. When he sat down on his Throne for the first time in all of Gladiator Village, they put the Crown on his head.

This was in the middle of the Third Age. Bat Head was the evil despicable King, and he provoked a War and caused how the War started. Bat Head sent some men and set Gladiator Village on fire. They did all kinds of horrible things that made the Villagers get very angry. Gladiator pulled out his Sword to kill Bat Head, but Bat Head had only sent the Army. Bat Head was not fighting in this War because he didn't want to die.

When the army of Bad Guys came and tore the celebration apart, a lot of the people felt sad and tormented. A lot of people wanted to retaliate and fight. They were trying to vote for this.

But the new Gladiator King said, "Do not get doubtful. We still have one chance. This is not the end of the world. I'm your new King so I will be able to help you. And don't worry, we'll get rid of those Bad Guys. I promise you, it won't happen again."

This cheered up some of the Villagers, but a lot of the Villagers still felt sad. Like Farmer George. He was only twenty-five years old. He was an Orphan.

Farmer George came up to the King holding his arms like a fist to his chest and knelt down in front of Gladiator very nicely. Farmer George looked up with fiery eyes and said to him, "I would like to join you and help you and the Village destroy Bat Head and his Bad Guys."

Then Gladiator looked at him with amazement. His eyes were shocked. His eyes were big. He pulled out his Sword and knighted him as Captain.

The person who was Captain was kicked
out, and George became Captain in his place.
The people began cheering up, even though a
lot of them still felt angry.

Chapter Two
The White Troll

Well, one day, there was this White Troll. He didn't used to be called the White Troll. He was just a Troll like every other Troll until the day he was lost in a snowstorm. He got so much snow on him that he remained white. His parents eventually found him, or he wouldn't be in the story, of course. He remained being called the White Troll, and he was destined for greatness.

He had a Quest. His first Quest was—well he didn't know what his first Quest was and the only way to find out was to go to the King of Masheebia, which is not a real word.

So he went to Masheebia, and as he walked up to the entrance he pulled out his Weapon just in case.

When the Guards saw him they said, "Halt!" They put their swords like an "X."

"I've come to look for a Quest," the White Troll stated.

"Well, I hope you're going to be okay. You'll probably risk losing your neck," replied the Guards.

The White Troll said, "I don't care. I could kill him."

So the Guards said, "Okay."

Then the White Troll walked over and saw some Candles. POP! BOOM! All the Candles popped up. He saw an Old Man with a Robe and a Hood. He also had a Staff. The Old Man, whose name was Masheebia, said, "Who's here?"

The White Troll replied, "The White Troll."

Then Masheebia said, "Go away."

But the White Troll said, "Wait. I'm here asking for a Quest."

Masheebia said, "Are you worthy of the Quest?"

"I've been worthy. I am worthy," replied the White Troll as he cleared his throat very nervously, and stood there sweating.

Finally Masheebia said, "Well, you will need lots and lots of training, and then you'll be ready for your first Quest." (I don't want to tell you what Masheebia said after that, or it would spoil the next two chapters).

After that, the White Troll was getting trained, until all he needed was one more day of training. Then the White Troll could face his Quest.

CHAPTER THREE
BAT HEAD

SO BAT HEAD was, of course, was doing everything he needed—rubbing his fat hands and looking at his General. They had captured a different Guy. They hadn't captured anybody important—he's not really one of the main characters. But this Guy was captured.

Bat Head, taking off his Gloves with a loud sound, asked his General, "Hey, what's up with this Prisoner?"

The General answered, "He's stubborn."

Then Bat Head said with a loud, demanding voice, "Bring him!"

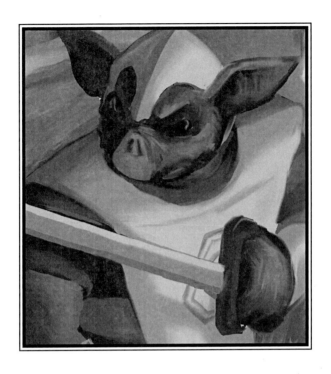

The Prisoner came with his head slouching down. Bat Head said, "We are looking for the White Troll. Have you seen him?"

The Prisoner went to a totally different subject because he didn't want to tell. But Bat Head stopped him immediately and said, "We are looking for a 'T' word. Where is the Troll?"

The Prisoner said, "I've been looking to investigate things that begin with the letter 'M.'"

Bat Head rolled his eyes and then said, "Put him back in Jail."

With very much annoyance Bat Head said, "What are we going to do?" He looked at his General with a very despicable look in his eyes. His eyebrows were out and he was almost looking like he was going to pull his ear off— but he wasn't—he was actually massaging his ear. Then he decided, "Hmm, we need to find this Troll, or should I say the White Troll, and destroy him."

The General warned him saying, "I've heard rumors that the White Troll is very dangerous."

But Bat Head said, "Are you crazy? I am the one who has plans. And I am going to capture somebody." (If I told you who, it would spoil the next chapter). He was so happy that he almost gave everybody Jewels—which he never does.

So Bat Head went and had a big Feast, and celebrated about the capture that he planned to have. But he had never faced the White Troll's wrath.

CHAPTER FOUR
THE CAPTURE OF GLADIATOR

ONE DAY THE Gladiator and his men, led by Captain George, were getting ready to face the Bad Guys, but he was not very happy about it because he was thinking he would probably get captured or die. But he scolded himself quickly before they heard him say the word, "Charge!" He got all his men ready, fixed his Armor up, and got his sharpest Sword. The only people who stayed behind were the ones who helped the injured.

Once King Gladiator said "Charge!" they had a fierce Battle. It was very bad. (So bad that if I told you how bloody and horrible it was, I think the grownups wouldn't let you read this book). The Good Guys lost—but don't worry, they'll come back. Gladiator got injured, which had never happened before—so that was kind of the reason they lost.

Bat Head's men captured the Gladiator, which was a big loss for the Good Guys because if the Good Guys didn't have the Gladiator they pretty much lost every Battle—and it was very rare that they would lose a Battle with the Gladiator.

Bat Head's men took the Gladiator to Jail.

Bat Head was sitting on his Throne talking to his General and saying stuff like, "Hey look, what's up with the Prisoner?"

The General answered with a yawn, "He's fine."

With an annoyed tone in his voice Bat Head said, "Bring him!"

Gladiator came in with his head looking straight at Bat Head with curiosity, his hands and feet in Chains. Bat Head said, "Do you know where the White Troll is?"

Gladiator went totally silent.

Bat Head screamed, "We are looking for the White Troll! Where is the White Troll?"

Gladiator remained silent and he was taken back to his Jail cell.

Again they brought Gladiator in and he was kind of moving and twitching, trying to get out of the Chains. But the Guards held on tightly.

Then Bat Head got down from his Throne and he ordered his Servant to bring him his Drink. He was very thirsty and very nervous to confront Gladiator.

He said to his Servant, "Drink!" The Servant brought Bat Head his Drink and he sipped it with a loud noise that made the Gladiator's ears pop.

Gladiator said, "Why are you capturing me?"

Bat Head's eyes were red and bloodshot. He almost looked like he was about to cry because he was so scared, but he decided not to show his embarrassment even a little.

Then Bat Head said, "Well, there's no one going to be saving you. You'll have to serve me or I'll put you in the Dungeon for at least ten days. If no one else saves you, or your rightful Hero, your Friend, the White Troll, doesn't come, we will have to tie you to a Pole and just kill you."

Gladiator looked at him and started to pull out his Dagger since one of his arms had come free. When he pulled it out and was about to throw it at Bat Head, the General pulled out his Sword and started fighting Gladiator.

The General won because Gladiator was in Chains, and plus the Guards had knocked out Gladiator with their Spears. It was an easy win for Bat Head and his Guards.

When Bat Head had had enough of this nonsense he said, "I've had enough of this nonsense," and he told his Guards to take all of Gladiator's Armor off and put him into rags. So they did that. All they gave him was a tiny little Dagger for his defense. That's it.

Then they put him to his knees, and while holding him really tightly Bat Head said to him, "When is the White Troll coming?"

Gladiator said, "I don't know. I don't know."

But Bat Head said quickly and loudly, "Liar! Take him away to the Dungeon for ten days."

And the Gladiator was dragged away yelling, "Please, please, I beg of you."

But Bat Head said, "No! Don't give him food or drink. Not even a crumb of bread."

And so the Gladiator was put in the Dungeon and he was very tormented, sad, and didn't get his hopes up because he thought it was hopeless. The only person who gave him any hope at all was the White Troll. Gladiator had known the White Troll for so long that he knew he was the only Friend brave enough to save him.

CHAPTER FIVE
THE DESPERATE SITUATION GLADIATOR IS IN

GLADIATOR WAS SITTING in the Dungeon with very little light. His head was slouching. His elbows were ripped up. His knees were skinned. His eyes were black as the night and bloodshot. And his Dagger was very small, but he tried not to lose hope.

But that was hard, especially when, once in a while, he would see one of Bat Head's Prisoners being taken out of the Prison to be executed. That was one of his worries; another was patiently waiting for the White Troll.

Sometimes he even screamed to get the Guard's attention and ask for food, but they would give him no food. So he was in a very bad position.

One of Gladiator's prisoner Friends snuck into a cell close by and was keeping him very comforted until it was his Friend's turn to be killed. It was a very bad time for the Gladiator because along with the White Troll, that was one of the best Friends he had ever had.

Even so, Gladiator encouraged his Friends. He said, "Don't worry. Something will come. Something has to come. If not, it's probably God's will. But something will come. I can feel it."

Then Gladiator and his Friends heard the Guards' footsteps and their conversation. Gladiator started to reach for his Dagger, but the Dungeon Chains stopped him. Gladiator sobbed and cried so hard that his tears almost flooded the Dungeon. Then they took another one of his Friends to be executed. They tortured his Friend so bad that his screams were so loud that the whole Kingdom could hear it.

Gladiator looked up to the one Window in his Cell so that the Light could shine on his face and said, "I'll never be saved. I will never be saved."

Chapter Six
How Scared Gladiator Was

So Gladiator was sitting across from the Window. He was shivering and getting colder. His heart was trembling, and he was getting more and more scared. It seemed that everything in the Dungeon was haunted. He could hear the rattling of Chains from the old Prisoners in the Chambers.

Gladiator was scared of his death, not of the Dungeon that much. It was himself that he was worried about. He thought no one would come. He was scared out of his brain. Even a little squeak of his Sandal would scare him. He didn't want anything to happen to him.

One day Gladiator heard Guards coming. He was so scared. He wanted to pull out his Dagger, but he was in Chains. This made him so frustrated that he tried to break free from the Chains with all his might.

When the Guards saw him they asked him, "What are you doing?"

He said, "Oh, nothing."

One of the Bad Guys came over. He had a missing eye with no eye patch. Gladiator was kind of smiling but in a scared kind of awkward way. The Guard said, "Why are you smiling?"

Gladiator said, "Why do you have a missing eye? I was looking at it." The Guard was very offended and he knocked Gladiator out, hitting him in the head. Once that happened, he thought Bat Head was going to kill him. He thought he only had three days left of life.

After the Gladiator was knocked out by the Guard with a missing eye he had a Dream of his rescue—some Troll coming in....

rescuing…. destroying Bat Head…. saving the day…. coming home with exciting things…. there was a huge Celebration…. and right before they were crowning Gladiator King and the White Troll Prince—POOF!!

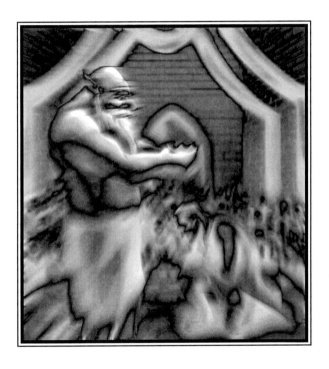

Gladiator woke up panting. The Dream kind of gave him more confidence, but he still was doubtful.

Chapter Seven
White Troll Worries and Plans the Rescue

THE WHITE TROLL was walking with a big thump. He was worrying a lot about how much time he had and what he was supposed to do. But he was planning in his worry. He was planning how he would get into the Dungeon, how he was supposed to fight Bat Head, and other details.

As the White Troll was walking to the Village where his Cousins lived, he suddenly bumped into Captain George, the Farmer from Gladiator's Kingdom who had become Gladiator's Captain.

The White Troll said, "Hey. Aren't you Gladiator's Captain?"

Captain George said, "You bet."

Just as the White Troll and Captain George were entering the Village the White Troll asked, "What are you doing in this Village?"

Captain George responded, "I'm not staying here; I'm on my way to find the Phoenix and ask him to send a Message to the Gladiator.

The White Troll said, "Good luck with that, and thanks for helping out."

Captain George said, "Helping out with what?"

The White Troll whispered, "I'm going to tell you a secret. My Quest is to save the Gladiator."

With that, Captain George waved goodbye, and the White Troll continued walking to his Cousins' house where he found his Cousins— Brown Troll and Black Troll. The reason they were called Black Troll and Brown Troll was because the Black Troll was lost in a black storm and the Brown Troll was lost in a brown desert storm.

The White Troll was very excited to see them; they were the best Planners of all in the land that they lived in—which was called

Magical Touch. Their planning skills would be very helpful to the White Troll on his Quest.

What the Cousin Trolls were planning was very good, but the White Troll still had so many worries—almost like Gladiator. He was trying not to give up. He would not give up. "I will continue the Quest that I've been given," he scolded himself very sternly.

He was so mad at himself that he banged the kitchen counter with his hand just as his Cousins came in. They got really scared so White Troll said, "It's an ant," so he wouldn't scare his Cousins.

After they had finished making their Plans, the White Troll waved good-bye, and walked pretty close to Bat Head's Dominion. He was still so worried. His faith was really strong so he scolded himself for worrying.

There was not one part when his Cousins had lied or spoiled his Plans. They were the most trustworthy Friends he'd ever had after his Father's death a couple billion years ago, and his Mother's sickness in 1912 at the Titanic. He knew that his Cousins were the most faithful, they were the most helpful, they were the most fun, and they were definitely the best at planning things.

They were also very good at encouraging the White Troll to keep on going and pushing through. All Trolls have special gifts when they have Cousins—trust, faith, hope, and endurance to finish a Quest. All this bolstered the White Troll's faith.

CHAPTER EIGHT
BAT HEAD'S DESPICABLE PLANS

BAT HEAD WAS in his backyard and then in his front yard. He was looking at a Map while his Warriors were sharpening their Weapons and doing all the stuff they need to do as Bad Guys.

Bat Head was talking with his General about the most despicable Plan they could do. They thought, "Hmmm, maybe if we put Gladiator on trial as Bait, then we could trap the White Troll while he's on his way coming to save the Gladiator from trial. The White Troll will be trying to save Gladiator from the Dungeon, which would be easy, but in the

Courtyard—that wouldn't be easy." So they decided to use Gladiator as Bait.

The General warned them that Trolls are the most fierce, biggest, and most dangerous Creatures of all the land.

But Bat Head just said, "Are you insane? I'm Bat Head—you're the General. We are the baddest Bad Guys and we can do it. Don't worry."

There was a lot of division amongst the Bad Guys. They continued questioning Bat Head; they knew he was going to fail— because fairytales, stories, and movies have Bad Guys die and get captured. The Bad Guys were trying to prevent that from happening, but Bat Head just kept going on with his despicable Plan.

Bat Head was talking to himself and he made a motion for his General to come into his room to talk privately.

When the General and Bat Head were talking in the Tent, the General said, "What if the Bait doesn't work?"

Then Bat Head said, "Maybe if we just kill my arch-enemy the Gladiator, then when the White Troll thinks he's still alive he'll come out. That's when we can capture and kill the White Troll, too."

Bat Head's eyes got very big. He had goose bumps and his knuckles were cracking as he said, "Prepare Gladiator for trial. It's time to bring him to his death."

CHAPTER NINE
WHITE TROLL FEARS HE MIGHT HAVE TO GIVE UP

SO THE WHITE Troll was doing his normal traveling, buying some food and all the supplies he needed to finish his Quest of saving his greatest Friend before trial.

One day he was walking in a Village called Lighteningly. In Lighteningly Village he saw a lot of people wearing Lighteningly Hats and eating Lighteningly Pears and other really weird things that we can't eat.

As the White Troll was walking out of Lighteningly Village he saw these weird Woods called Lighteningly Woods. He walked in suspiciously, trying not to touch the Trees for fear he'd go.... PING.... and be electrocuted.

As he was walking on the ground the White Troll found this nice area that had a little bit of Electrocuting Grass and some Electrocuting Peaches so he sat down on a Blanket so he wouldn't get electrocuted.

He pulled out some food and started eating it, but as he was eating it he finally realized it was a weird Pear. It made him want to go home right away. He was mumbling and talking to himself, "Should I give up? What if I don't make it? What if I die there? What will I do?" He was getting really, really, really, REALLY afraid.

The next morning when the White Troll got up he said, "I'm going back home," and he started walking back to Lighteningly Village. But when he stepped into Lighteningly Village he decided, "Hmm. I've been given a Quest to save a Friend and I shall finish the Quest that I have been given."

As he turned around, the White Troll started shaking in his boots. (But before he could shake in his boots he had to get some boots—in his size of course).

He had been walking around and around to the point he had gone into Demon-Tormenting Forest.

When the White Troll had come out of Lighteningly Villiage, he realized that he had been so scared and so distracted that he had forgotten to read the Sign that had the horrible name labeled on it. He had been walking uncautiously, not knowing what he was doing. He had been skipping along, breaking some Trees down, you know, like Trolls do.

Then the White Troll thought he heard a Demon voice. It sounded very scary and said, "I want you."

The White Troll was stuck and kind of frozen. He was almost going to faint, but he managed to keep his balance. Then a giant Demon came down.

The White Troll pulled out a Sword and beat it up as hard as he could. He tied it to the trunk of a tree, and grabbed it by the neck saying, "Okay, Buddy, or should I say Enemy, tell me the way to Bat Head's Castle."

The Demon said in a choking voice, "I don't know. I don't know," and he was laughing rather oddly.

Then the White Troll choked him very hard to get him to spit out the way to Bat Head's castle.

"Alright, take it easy, boy. It's ...." And then the White Troll saw a little Vision of Bat Head's Castle. It was still very far away. (I can't tell you how close, or else I'd spoil the next few chapters).

Bat Head still had worries, but he didn't give up.

CHAPTER TEN
ONLY TWO DAYS TO LIVE

GLADIATOR, OF COURSE, was in the Dungeon saying to himself, "I'm going to die and there's no hope. This story's only going to end with tears." All the Guards were kind of laughing at him and cussing at him.

One time, the Bad Guys were so stupid they said, "Maybe we don't have to keep the Gladiator captured in the Dungeon."

So Bat Head said, "Okay. Bring him out." It was kind of funny that the Bad Guys would do that, but don't worry—they put him back in Jail. Let me tell you how.

The Gladiator still had some Friends still being held captive. When the Bad Guys came to take Gladiator out of the Dungeon, one of his Friends said, "We will accept the most gracious offer from Bat Head." Bat Head was letting them leave, although they didn't have a good chance of escaping. Gladiator had a feeling this was a Trick.

Gladiator and his Friends appeared before Bat Head who said, "Bring your little Princess, too!" He meant the White Troll—which was very insulting.

Gladiator, whose hands were finally free from Chains, reached into the folds of his clothing and pulled out his Dagger. He threw it but Bat Head's General deflected it with his Sword just in time. So the Bad Guys put the Gladiator back into the Dungeon.

Gladiator only had two days left to live, and so it seemed like Gladiator's doom. He was so furious he felt like punching the iron bars in his Cell, which he couldn't do because he was back in Chains. He had tried so hard and still nothing had worked out. All he could say to himself was, "I've only got two days to live."

CHAPTER ELEVEN
THE WHITE TROLL STRUGGLES

THE WHITE TROLL was walking around washing his Swords and giant Weapons that of course cannot be held by anyone unless they had Troll strength.

After that, he headed to a Stable called Crazy Stable. He walked in and saw this Guy staying with the Horses. He also saw eighteen hundred bottles of Wine next to him.

The White Troll said, "Sir, could I please borrow a Horse?"

The Guy looked at the White Troll with a look that said, "Who are you?" kind of a thing and said, "I wish I could but I got things to do. I got to bathe myself and drink more Wine."

The White Troll knocked the Guy out so he could find a Horse because he knew a drunk Guy could make some Trolls struggle.

Then the White Troll realized he couldn't ride the Horse—his weight was too big for Horses. So he had to walk—right through the Mud Swamp.

He was walking and struggling. There were evil Birds and Demons and all those kinds of bad things. They were tearing his skin, cussing, and hurting him. It would take a whole day to get through the Mud Swamp—many people don't ever get through the Mud Swamp.

Suddenly the White Troll just blacked out.

When the White Troll woke up everything was dark. It was very dark. Probably even scarier for it was night, I believe. He was walking and walking and walking—it almost seemed like he was walking in circles. And he was because he kept taking the same path!

He said to himself, "Oh White Troll, you Pighead. Use your Brain! It's left. Wait. Right. Left—right—left—right. Eeny, meeny, miney, mo. Right. Okay."

So the White Troll went right and soon he found a Mud Turtle. The White Troll said, "Please tell me which way to go."

The Mud Turtle replied, "I don't care."

The White Troll said, "If you don't tell me, our whole world will die and you will, too."

Again the Mud Turtle said, "I don't care," and all he would say was, "I don't care." This made the White Troll roar so loud that the Mud Turtle had to give the answer.

Once the White Troll got out of the Mud Swamp, he found himself fighting in a War with Barbarians that had come back to life. He was weak and feeble, and he was struggling in the War because the Barbarians were so dangerous and insane. He struggled and struggled and struggled and struggled. His skin was all cut up and he had black eyes. He only had one Weapon left and he was very weak.

Suddenly he came upon a nice place. It was decent and he said, "Whew!" He was panting and he went to his knees. "Oh my word! Why did I even come on this Quest?" He was regretting everything he had done, thinking thoughts like, "I wonder if maybe the Gladiator might be dead by now." He struggled so badly.

Then the White Troll heard something go "Eeech!"

"What in the heck is that?" he wondered. He turned around and saw the creepiest thing you'd ever see. It was the King Demon, and as the White Troll opened his Pack and pulled out his last Sword, he gulped really loud and uttered, "Glump." He was shaking and sweating.

The Demon said, "What brings you into my evil presence?"

The White Troll was trembling as he gripped his little Weapon and sarcastically said, "I'm just taking a tour."

The Demon looked at him really bored and said, "Okay, let's just fight." And the

White Troll hit him. The Demon was hurt very badly.

Then the White Troll went into the Beautiful Green Garden saying to himself, "I'm so green I'll never make it. These stories always end with struggle after struggle."

And so he struggled.

CHAPTER TWELVE
THE WHITE TROLL IS ENCOURAGED
BY THE PHOENIX

So AFTER THE big struggle the White Troll found this very nice place—very decent with stuff that a lot of kids and adults would like to sleep in—not like a hotel, or anything. He went inside and he saw something that went BAMM! It was absolutely beautiful! His heart was beating really fast. He dropped everything. His eyes were really big. And then he realized it was a Phoenix Guard.

"This must be the Palace of the Phoenixes," thought the White Troll.

He turned to one of the Phoenix Guards and said, "I would like to speak with the King Phoenix." He knew the Phoenix was a great Encourager in all the land of Nakia—that's the land they lived in.

But the Phoenix Guard said, "The King Phoenix doesn't see White Trolls, especially you. You look particularly dangerous."

The White Troll said, "Well, I'm here to save the Gladiator."

The Phoenix Guard began laughing, and said, "You? You?"

Then the Phoenix Guard remembered that if a White Troll was insulted he would get angry, so they decided to call the King.

The Phoenix King came out demanding, "What's going on here?" And then he saw the White Troll.

The Phoenix King brought the White Troll inside and they had a talk. The White Troll asked, "What do you think I should do? I think I should give up. I'm not doing so well."

The Phoenix King answered, "Come on. You've been given a Quest. You should do it. I know you're a great Warrior and I know you've done well. You've survived humongous struggles. You've made it this far. You can't give up. You've done very, very well."

The White Troll was very encouraged.

The White Troll heard a voice, and as he turned to his right he saw someone he was very glad to see again. It was Captain George! He was wearing leather Armor with a Sword and Sheath attached to his left side. He was holding his Helmet by his right side.

The White Troll said, "Aren't you here to deliver a message to the Phoenix?"

Captain George said, "Of course. I'm here just as I told you I would be."

"How long have you been here?" the White Troll asked.

Captain George responded, "Only three days; the Phoenix King is already busy making arrangements to visit the Gladiator."

Then the Phoenix King said, "Hmm, we shall have a Council about this later."

Soon they went to the Phoenix Meeting Room. Everybody sat down and at first the

White Troll was talking and sharpening his Blade until the King Phoenix walked in and said, "Silence! Attention!"

They all sat down quietly. The Phoenix King didn't see a Phoenix Guard right where he was going to sit, so he accidentally sat on the Phoenix Guard who began screaming, "Ahhh…. Ahhh…. Ahhh!"

The Phoenix King said, "I'm sorry, my little Friend."

Then they all talked and encouraged the White Troll saying, "You're a great Guy. You can do this because you're a very great Troll." They encouraged him very well.

The King Phoenix, who was the best of all in Nakia, then spoke the last best thing, "When a Knight or a Troll is given a Quest, he must not give up." He encouraged the White Troll to persevere through his struggles, and gave him a poison Sword. This gave the White Troll confidence.

Later on the Phoenix King said, "Want to spend the night?"

But the White Troll said, "No," and kind of blocked their beds. So they all continued doing everything they had been doing until the White Troll became more confident and started thinking of only encouraging things.

Then the Queen Phoenix came out and said, "The White Troll?"

He came over to her and bowed. She said, "Stay here now and I'll tell you what to do." They all encouraged him to stay one more day and they had a very good time.

When it was finally time for the White Troll to leave he was given a Package—some new Weapons and some food for along the way just in case he was starving to death.

He walked away with a good wave—a long wave that almost blew all the trees off, it was so big. He included a special goodbye wave to Captain George.

As the White Troll walked away, the Queen Phoenix gave him a Ball. She told him that if he would blink and the Ball turned blue, it meant that his Quest was done and it was time for him to go home.

When the White Troll left—blink, blink—the Ball did turn blue, and he stopped to consider what he was to do. He wondered, "Does that mean my job is done?"

So he went back, but the King Phoenix said, "That was a Test—to test if you're going to finish or not." It was a good lesson for the White Troll, and passing the Test helped him very much.

And so finally, the White Troll walked away and headed to Bat Head's Castle.

Chapter Thirteen
The Phoenix Visits the Gladiator

GLADIATOR WAS LOOKING out towards his tiny Dungeon window hoping that something would happen right as the Phoenix was flying towards the Dungeon window—until he saw there were some Guards on the Watchtower.

As the Phoenix was making some amazing flying maneuvers to outsmart the Guards, the Gladiator spotted him and continued watching him until he flew right through his tiny window.

Gladiator was hoping that the Phoenix was going to break him out of the Dungeon. He said, "Can you save me?"

The Phoenix responded, "No, but I'm here to give you some encouragement."

Gladiator looked disappointed. The Phoenix said, "It's okay. Someone's coming. Someone's coming to help you. I promise you if they try to destroy you, I won't let that happen."

Gladiator rolled his eyes, so the Phoenix continued, "Let me give you a Clue that will help you solve who your Rescuer is. He's white as snow. He is as strong as ten men, and bigger than a grizzly bear." Then the Phoenix disappeared in the blink of an eye.

The Gladiator tried to figure out who his Rescuer might be. He thought and thought. "I'm sure I know someone who is white as snow, as strong as ten men, and bigger than a grizzly bear." It took him a couple of hours, but he figured it out. It was the White Troll.

Right then and there he knelt down and prayed. That gave Gladiator hope, which gave him strength.

He still had worries, but he knew his Friend, the White Troll, was on his way to rescue him.

Chapter Fourteen
Gladiator's Last Day

Now Gladiator was wondering how many hours he had left. He wasn't counting so good. He had kind of forgotten how to count numbers because he had been in Jail for so long. He was really struggling a lot.

Then Gladiator heard these Guards laughing and giggling, and coming downstairs loudly. All of the Prisoners got up, stood very straight, and saluted them because when Guards come down in Bat Head's Palace you have to salute. If you don't salute them, they'll kill you. Even Gladiator saluted them, although he had a frown on his face because he didn't want to.

One of the Guards said, "Hey Gladiator. Have you heard?"

Gladiator responded, "No."

Then they said, "This is your last day."

"Why?" he responded.

They said, "You're up, so be prepared, Gladiator. You're not a Hero."

Then they tricked Gladiator by saying the White Troll had died. It was only a trick, but they wanted Gladiator to have no hope so they made it sound hopeless. Then they took him to Bat Head.

Bat Head commanded the Guards, "Prepare Gladiator!" So the Guards took Gladiator. Bat Head said, "Whip him!" So they whipped him until his shirt was ripped.

Gladiator's back was bleeding from the lines the Guard's whips had made on it. Gladiator barely heard Bat Head say, "This is your last day. So be prepared."

It was a very hard day for Gladiator. They didn't give him breakfast or lunch. And for dinner, Gladiator was given worms and spider legs to eat, and worm blood to drink.

They were very unkind to him. They actually wanted him to die on his last day, but he lived because the Phoenix gave up his last living Power for the Gladiator.

It made Bat Head very angry that the Gladiator had survived his last day.

Chapter Fifteen
The Big Rescue

GLADIATOR WAS STILL sitting in the Dungeon waiting for a Sign, waiting for something to happen as he had been waiting for most of this story.

The Guards came down the stairs again laughing. Gladiator then remembered he had his invisible Sword by his side, which he was unable to get until they took him out of his Chains.

As he was being dragged, the Prisoners stood up and saluted the Guards so they wouldn't die—Bat Head's demand because he liked his Guards almost as much as he liked himself.

The Guards mockingly reminded Gladiator that this was his last day, to which Gladiator sarcastically replied, "Oh, that's very nice!"

They just continued taking him from the Dungeon to Bat Head.

Eagerly Bat Head immediately commanded his guards, "Whip him!" Gladiator was whipped again, and they tortured him with all kinds of horrible things.

Bat Head's next command was, "Bring him up for trial!"

As the Guards took Gladiator outside, he asked them again if the White Troll was still alive. "No! He's not alive," they lied.

Meanwhile, the White Troll was coming back from the Phoenix's Palace and up to Bat Head's Castle. The Guards at the Gate were sleeping, so the White Troll tipped toed, but when he tipped toed he ended up making a loud sound because his feet were so big and the Guards woke up.

The White Troll knocked them out, took their Armor, and put it on himself. The Armor really didn't fit him, but the other Guards didn't notice. They just thought the White Troll was a really strong Guard.

The White Troll entered the Palace very cautiously and suspiciously until he realized it was empty. He looked out a window and saw a Crowd. Gladiator was tied up on a Pole.

The White Troll knew exactly what was going to happen so he went running out the door, grabbed his Weapon, the poison Sword that the King Phoenix had given him and demanded, "Bat Head, let him go!"

Bat Head just laughed and said to his Guards, "Men, get him!"

At that exact moment, Captain George arrived and came to the roof of the Castle Tower. He looked down to see if the White Troll and Gladiator needed his help.

Suddenly he heard a plop and it was boots. He turned around and pulled out his Sword. There was the Bat Head's General, shirtless, but wearing his shoulder-spiked Cape. He had grayish black hair with a white beard.

Bat Head's General said with a snarl, "Well, Captain George, I see it is about time we fought each other."

Captain George did not immediately respond because he knew that responding to the mocking of him wouldn't do any good.

Finally Captain George said, "I don't want to fight you; all I want to do is help the Gladiator and the White Troll be free. That's all I want to do."

The General responded, "Well if you want that, you will have to fight me."

Captain George sighed. He remembered that a long time ago he and the General were good Friends—until the General got mad because Captain George had married Alexandria, and the General was also in love with her. Ever since then, the General had been plotting revenge to kill Captain George. There is a lot of history that I haven't told about these people, but I will later.

When Captain George pulled out his Sword, he walked back and forth pointing his Sword but not even moving it. The General slowly took out two Swords from his two sided sheaths and he waved them. The fight began.

Captain George and the General were fighting for a long time. Captain George was hoping he could kill the General before the Gladiator and the White Troll needed help.

They fought and fought. Then suddenly the General cut a little bit of Captain George's rib. Captain George reacted and cut the General's arm. The General didn't give up. He grabbed a Dagger and threw it right at Captain George's legs. Captain George removed it from his leg and threw it at the General's shoulder.

The General was very very tired, as was Captain George. They had been fighting for hours. The General removed the Dagger from his shoulder and threw it down the Castle Tower.

Then suddenly, in one swift motion the General did a flip and cut Captain George's back in one big slash. Captain George fell to the ground in pain. Right as the General was about to cut Captain George's head off, Captain George did a backflip and stabbed the General right in the back. His Sword went through the General.

The General had one last thing that he did, but to understand this, I will have to give you some back-story. The General and Captain George were Friends as kids. They had given each other tiny Weapons that they promised to keep forever. The General kept his, not because he wanted to remember the Friendship, but for fighting emergencies only. However, Captain George kept his Weapon as a remembrance of how he and the General were Friends. Captain George's Weapon was a small kid-size Mace, and he only used it to help people. The General's Weapon was a tiny Axe, the size a kid would carry.

It was this tiny Weapon that the General pulled out from its sheath that was tied into the folds of his Cape right as Captain George stabbed him in the back.

The General threw it, and it launched right at Captain George's stomach. The slash was big. It took a lot of willpower for Captain George to look down at what was happening.

Blood darkened his shirt immediately, and Captain George felt the warmth and the sting. Painfully, he took the Axe out and dropped it. As Captain George fell to the ground, he looked over at the General who had also slumped to the ground.

Meanwhile, Bat Head's men were attacking the White Troll, but the Guards were of no use because they were not as skilled as the

White Troll who had planned and prepared for this moment.

Bat Head, who had been watching the fight, was backing up nervously and backed up right into Gladiator's invisible Sword. Bat Head looked at his Guard who was still fighting and said, "Stop, I will handle this matter myself." He cracked his fingers and went over to Gladiator. He took the invisible Sword off Gladiator, and the Sword that signified Gladiator as King instantly became visible.

Bat Head said to the White Troll, "Okay White Troll, you've made it far. You maneuvered getting help from your Cousins, you made it through Demon-Tormenting Forest, and you managed to get Power from the Phoenix. You even made it through Masheebia somehow. So now I'm giving you a choice. You can either leave, or Gladiator dies."

The White Troll responded, "I pick neither. Neither one is an option."

Bat Head pointed the Sword closer to Gladiator's neck. The White Troll said, "Oh look, there is a Commoner beating up your Guard."

As Bat Head turned to look, the White Troll hit him.... PANG!.... right in Bat Head's head. Bat Head fell to the ground.

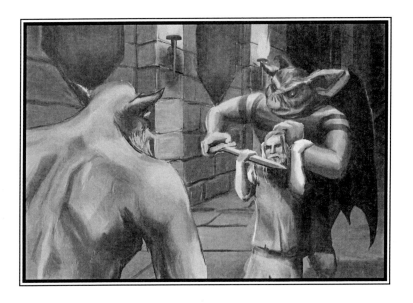

The White Troll untied the Gladiator and they stormed out toward the Castle Gate quicker than you can say, "A bunch of munchy, crunchy carrots!" Just as they were about to leave the Castle, Bat Head jumped in front of them and pulled out Gladiator's Sword.

It was a brilliant battle. There was a lot that happened. Gladiator had a hard time fighting because he was weak from all the whipping Bat Head's men had done to him.

The White Troll's Weapon was knocked out of his hands as he moved closer to help Gladiator. As they were fighting, Bat Head used Gladiator's Sword and stabbed Gladiator!

Fortunately Gladiator didn't die and was okay. The White Troll hit Bat Head's arm so hard that Bat Head dropped Gladiator's Sword. Gladiator and the White Troll were so alarmed that they picked up Gladiator's Sword and they both held the Sword together. They both stabbed Bat Head right at the same time!

Once Bat Head was dead, all his remaining Guards fled back to Lighteningly Village, and the Commoners were finally free.

As the White Troll and the Gladiator were high-fiving, Gladiator said, "Finally, it's over, we did it. This is what we've been waiting for."

Suddenly they turned around, and out of the corner of their eyes they saw a hand—Captain George was lying on the ground. They quickly ran up the Tower and climbed out on the Castle roof.

The General was lying there dead. Gladiator pulled the Sword from his back, and went quickly over to Captain George. The Axe wound was very bad and he was losing blood really fast.

Gladiator quickly ripped both sleeves off of his ragged shirt and tied them together. It was just long enough to wrap around Captain George's wound.

Using his great Strength, the White Troll carried Captain George, while Gladiator found two good Horses outside the Castle Wall. Together they rode back home to Gladiator Village.

Captain George successfully lived. The Doctors in the land had great Powers and could heal almost every injury, so it was pretty easy for them to heal Captain George's wounds.

Captain George was happy to stand side by side with the Gladiator and the White Troll.

Now there is a secret I haven't told you this whole time. The last thing Bat Head said before he died was an awkward Riddle. No one knew what it meant. He said, "A next generation will come. I will kill my Brother. Once it is done, you will die."

To help you understand these last words from Bat Head, I will tell you that Bat Head and Gladiator are Brothers.

The reason Gladiator had been given the Throne, even though he was younger, was because he was more prepared. Bat Head, of course, just wanted control, control, and more control. Gladiator had more peace, but time was needed for Bat Head to get proper skills to become King—and this was how Bat Head repaid Gladiator.

Three years later, Captain George told Gladiator and the White Troll the Riddle Bat Head had spoken as his last words. They wrote it down and finally figured it out—the next generation of Bat Head was going to try and kill the next generation of Gladiator and the next generation of the White Troll. (But that story will be told in the sequel).

From that day forward, the Gladiator was the happiest King you could imagine, and the Villagers were happy that Captain George had helped the Gladiator King keep his promise to help them.

The White Troll successfully completed his Quest and was a Hero, a Hero beyond belief. He did other amazing Quests that are not told in this tale.

And they lived happily ever after in the Magical Land of Gladiator's Kingdom that they lived in.

THE END.